Geronimo Stilton
ENGLISH!

5 MY CLOTHES 我的衣服

新雅文化事業有限公司
www.sunya.com.hk

Geronimo Stilton English
MY CLOTHES 我的衣服

作　　者：Geronimo Stilton 謝利連摩・史提頓
譯　　者：申倩
責任編輯：王燕參
封面繪圖：Giuseppe Facciotto
插圖繪畫：Claudio Cernuschi, Andrea Denegri, Daria Cerchi
內文設計：Angela Ficarelli, Raffaella Picozzi
出　　版：新雅文化事業有限公司
　　　　　香港筲箕灣耀興道3號東匯廣場9樓
　　　　　營銷部電話：（852）2562 0161
　　　　　客戶服務部電話：（852）2976 6559
　　　　　傳真：（852）2597 4003
　　　　　網址：http://www.sunya.com.hk
　　　　　電郵：marketing@sunya.com.hk
發　　行：香港聯合書刊物流有限公司
　　　　　香港新界大埔汀麗路36號中華商務印刷大廈3字樓
　　　　　電話：（852）2150 2100　傳真：（852）2407 3062
　　　　　電郵：info@suplogistics.com.hk
印　　刷：C & C Offset Printing Co.,Ltd
　　　　　香港新界大埔汀麗路36號
版　　次：二〇一一年二月初版
　　　　　10 9 8 7 6 5 4 3 2 1

CONTENTS
目錄

BENJAMIN'S CLASSMATES

班哲文的老師和同學們

Maestra Topitilla
托比蒂拉・德・托比莉斯

Rarin
拉琳

Diego
迪哥

Rupa
露芭

Tui
杜爾

David
大衞

Sakura
櫻花

Mohamed
穆哈麥德

Tian Kai
田凱

Oliver
奧利佛

Milenko
米蘭哥

Trippo
特里普

Carmen
卡敏

Atina
阿提娜

Esmeralda
愛絲梅拉達

Pandora
潘朵拉

Takeshi
北野

Kuti
菊花

Benjamin
班哲文

Hsing
阿星

Laura
羅拉

Kiku
奇哥

Antonia
安東妮婭

Liza
麗莎

GERONIMO AND HIS FRIENDS
謝利連摩和他的家鼠朋友們

謝利連摩・史提頓 Geronimo Stilton
一個古怪的傢伙，簡直可以說是一隻笨拙的文化鼠。他是《鼠民公報》的總裁，正花盡心思改變報紙業的歷史。

菲・史提頓 Tea Stilton
謝利連摩的妹妹，她是《鼠民公報》的特派記者，同時也是一個運動愛好者。

班哲文・史提頓 Benjamin Stilton
謝利連摩的小侄兒，常被叔叔稱作「我的小乳酪」，是一隻感情豐富的小老鼠。

潘朵拉・華之鼠 Pandora Woz
柏蒂・活力鼠的小侄女、班哲文最好的朋友，是一隻活潑開朗的小老鼠。

柏蒂・活力鼠 Patty Spring
美麗迷人的電視新聞工作者，致力於她熱愛的電視事業。

賴皮 Trappola
謝利連摩的表弟，非常喜歡食物，風趣幽默，是一隻饞嘴、愛開玩笑的老鼠，善於將歡樂傳遞給每一隻鼠。

麗萍姑媽 Zia Lippa
謝利連摩的姑媽，對鼠十分友善，又和藹可親，只想將最好的給身邊的鼠。

艾拿 Iena
謝利連摩的好朋友，充滿活力，熱愛各項運動，他希望能把對運動的熱誠傳給謝利連摩。

史奎克・愛管閒事鼠 Ficcanaso Squitt
謝利連摩的好朋友，是一個非常有頭腦的私家偵探，總是穿着一件黃色的乾濕褸。

LET'S GET DRESSED!
一起來穿衣服！

親愛的小朋友，我們又見面了！我以一千塊莫澤雷勒乳酪發誓，我有一個特別好的消息要告訴你……今天我們要學習穿在我們身上的衣服的英文名稱！不但有我的衣服，還有我小姪兒班哲文的，潘朵拉的，柏蒂的，我的朋友們的，還有老鼠島上最有名的報紙《鼠民公報》的職員們的衣服。努力啊，讓我們一起來學習吧！

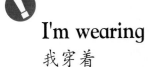

I'm wearing
我穿着

跟我謝利連摩・史提頓一起學英文，就像玩遊戲一樣簡單好玩！

你可以一邊看着圖畫一邊讀。
以下有幾個標誌，你要特別留意：

🧀 當看到 💿 標誌時，你可以聽CD，一邊聽，一邊跟着朗讀，還可以跟着一起唱歌。

🧀 當看到 ⭐ 標誌時，你可以和朋友們一起玩遊戲，或者嘗試回答問題。題目很簡單，它們對鞏固你所學過的內容很有幫助。

🧀 當看到 ❗ 標誌時，你要注意看一下格子裏的生字，反覆唸幾遍，掌握發音。

最後，不要忘記完成小測驗和練習冊裏的問題！看看你有多聰明吧。

祝大家學得開開心心！

謝利連摩・史提頓

> *Hello, I'm wearing my raincoat.*

CLOTHES 各式各樣的衣物

今天我的工作非常忙綠，不能陪班哲文和潘朵拉去公園玩了，所以把他們帶到了辦公室。班哲文和潘朵拉想跟大家玩一個遊戲：他們請《鼠民公報》的職員們用英語介紹自己穿的是什麼衣服，你也跟着一起說說看。

a pair of
一對

This is my tie and this is my jacket.

I'm wearing a pair of trousers and a sports jacket.

I'm wearing a suit and a waistcoat.

I'm wearing a pair of trousers and a shirt.

I'm wearing a skirt and a sweater.

I'm wearing a miniskirt and a jersey.

This is my hat and this is my raincoat.

This is my blouse.

I'm wearing a cardigan.

This is my bag.

This is my coat.

I'm wearing a pair of boots.

I'm wearing a pair of shoes.

⭐ 1. 謝利連摩穿的是什麼衣服呢？試着用英語説出來。

⭐ 2. 謝利連摩的外套是什麼顏色的？請用英語回答。

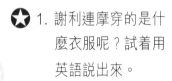

A FASHION PHOTO REPORT
時裝表演報告

菲是個特派記者，她剛剛為一個運動服裝表演拍照回來。她拍的照片真漂亮啊！潘朵拉一邊看着這些照片，一邊問菲這些衣服的英文名稱怎麼說，這真是一個學習的好機會啊⋯⋯你也跟着一起說說看。

Congratulations! These photos are very interesting.

What's this? What's that?

 these 這些

This is a T-shirt.

This is a sweatshirt.

This is a tracksuit.

This is a pair of casual trousers.

This is a pair of shorts.

This is a leotard.

This is a pair of jeans.

This is a pair of tennis shoes.

This is a pair of socks.

This is a judo suit.

This is a bike helmet.

This is an anorak.

DO YOU LIKE...?
你喜歡……嗎？

菲拍的照片真漂亮！我以一千塊莫澤雷勒乳酪發誓，《鼠民公報》的時尚雜誌這次一定會大獲成功。這時，在《鼠民公報》的辦公室裏，大家談論的惟一話題就是「時裝」！

Do you like my trousers?

Yes, I do.

Do you like my new shirt?

Yes, I do.

班哲文找到菲拍的另外一些照片，他和潘朵拉一邊看，一邊學習這些衣服的英文詞彙，你也跟着一起說說看。

a pair of trousers

a pair of shorts

a pair of jeans

a pair of tennis shoes

a pair of shoes

Do you like...?
你喜歡……嗎？
Yes, I do!
我喜歡。

★ 看看左邊的圖畫，你喜歡哪雙鞋子？哪條褲子？請用英語回答。

KIDS CLOTHES 童裝

菲把她在兒童時裝表演上拍的照片拿給班哲文和潘朵拉看，他們非常感興趣！他們一邊看照片，一邊問菲這些童裝衣服的英文名稱怎麼說，你也跟着一起說說看。

He's wearing a T-shirt.

She's wearing a dress.

dungarees

tracksuit

sweatshirt and jeans

shirt

T-shirt

anorak

dress

skirt

shorts

scarf

socks

shoes

boots

belt and cap

⭐ 1. 菲拿着的照片中的小朋友穿的是什麼衣服？它們是什麼顏色的？請指着照片中小朋友的衣服，用英語回答。

⭐ 2. 有人在椅子上放了一件衣服，這件衣服的英文名稱是什麼？

答案：

1. The boy is wearing an orange T-shirt and a pair of blue jeans. The girl is wearing a pink dress.

2. sweatshirt

12

Who Is Wearing a Blue Dress Today?

Who is wearing a blue dress today?
She is wearing a blue dress today!
Who is she? Who is she?
She is Rarin! She is Rarin!
Who is wearing a pair of jeans today?
He is wearing a pair of jeans today!
Who is he? Who is he?
He is Oliver! He is Oliver!
We are nice boys and we wear a T-shirt.
We are nice girls and we wear a T-shirt.
Who is wearing a green T-shirt today?
She is wearing a green T-shirt today!
Who is she? Who is she?
She is Pandora! She is Pandora!
We are nice boys and we wear a T-shirt.
We are nice girls and we wear a T-shirt.
Who is wearing dungarees today?
He is wearing dungarees today!
Who is he? Who is he?
He is Trippo! He is Trippo!

| his | 他的 |
| her | 她的 |

★ 有人在掛衣架上掛了一條圍巾，圍巾的英文名稱是什麼？

答案：scarf

請你跟着班哲文和潘朵拉一起用英語說出他們的朋友穿的是什麼衣服吧！

He's wearing a green belt. His cap is yellow.

She's wearing a blue skirt. Her T-shirt is pink.

13

THE LAUNDRY 洗衣服

我剛剛完成了一項重要的工作，於是趁着空閒時間，帶班哲文和潘朵拉一起去探望麗萍姑媽。這時，麗萍姑媽正在院子裏晾衣服。但是⋯⋯她所有的衣服都染紅了！哎，原來她忘記把白色內衣和別的有顏色的衣服分開來洗！我連忙安慰她說，這種事情經常發生在我身上！我常常把我的內衣染成綠色呢。

I'm sorry. You have to wash these clothes again.

underpants

knickers

tights

vest

laundry basket

Oh, no! I have to do my washing again.

Can I help you?

Can I help you?

⭐ 1. 洗衣籃的英文名稱是什麼？

班哲文和潘朵拉一起幫助麗萍姑媽晾衣服，
他們一邊晾衣服，一邊用英語說出衣服的名稱。
你也跟著一起說說看。

I have to 　我必須
can 　能夠
Can I help you? 我能夠幫你嗎？

help 　幫忙
again 　再一次

washing line

dressing gown

pajamas

slippers

clothes-horse

washing machine

iron

ironing board

⭐ 2. 麗萍姑媽用什麼電
器來洗衣服？請用
英語回答。

答案：
1. laundry basket
2. washing machine

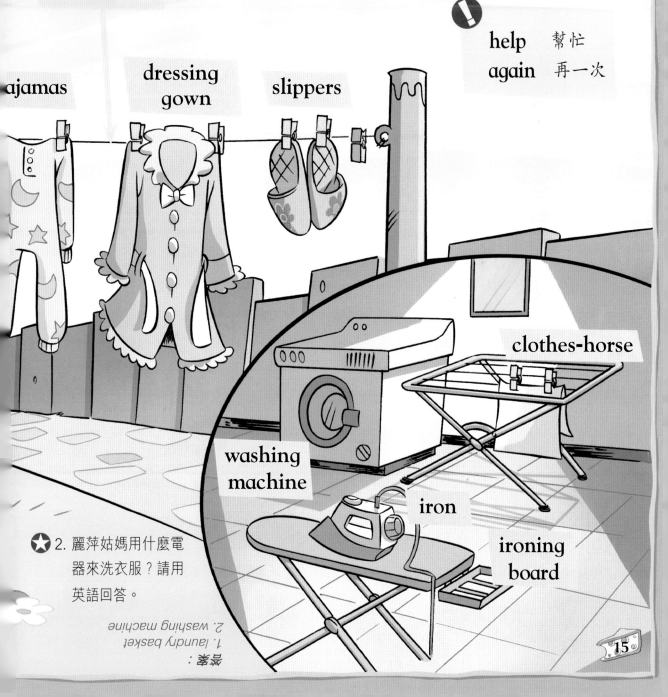

15

LET'S PLAY TOGETHER!
大家一起玩！

菲和賴皮也來找麗萍姑媽了。當菲、麗萍姑媽和我在一邊聊天的時候，賴皮跟班哲文和潘朵拉一起玩脫鞋子穿衣服的遊戲！他們一邊玩，還一邊說出衣物的名稱呢，你也跟著一起說說看。

This is the way I put on my scarf.

This is the way I take off my scarf.

This is the way I put on my cap.

This is the way I take off my cap.

This is the way I put on my sweatshirt.

This is the way I take off my sweatshirt.

This is the way I put on my coat.

This is the way I take off my coat.

put on	穿上
take off	脫掉

請你跟著班哲文和潘朵拉一起讀出下面的句子。你可以一邊讀，一邊跟著做動作。

Put on your socks!

Put on your shoes!

Take off your shoes!

Take off your socks!

All Day Long

This is the way I put on my shoes,
put on my shoes, put on my shoes,
this is the way I put on my shoes.
All day long!
This is the way I take off my shoes,
take off my shoes, take off my shoes,
this is the way I take off my shoes.
All day long!

This is the way
these are my shoes
I take off and put on my shoes.
All day long!
This is the way you put on your boots,
you take off your boots.
All day long!
You put on your boots, you take off your boots.
All day long!
This is the way
these are your boots
you take off and put on
your boots.
All day long!

聽完歌後，請你跟着班哲文和潘朵拉一起讀出下面的句子。你可以一邊讀，
一邊跟着做動作。

Put on your hat!

Put on your scarf!

Take off your scarf!

Take off your cap!

17

FASHION SHOW 時裝表演

班哲文、潘朵拉、菲和賴皮上了閣樓，這裏有一個衣櫃和一個箱子，麗萍姑媽用它們來存放一些不合穿的衣服，它們不是太小了就是太大了。班哲文和潘朵拉從箱子裏掏出衣服來扮演一場時裝表演，菲和賴皮則充當司儀介紹着他們所穿的衣服。你也跟着賴皮和菲一起用英語介紹這些衣服吧！

He's wearing a white shirt, a blue tie and a pair of yellow trousers.

She's wearing a green jacket, a pink blouse, a long brown skirt and a pair of red shoes.

He's wearing a purple T-shirt, a black waistcoat, an orange coat and a pair of red trousers.

She's wearing a grey dress, a white cardigan and a pair of blue shoes.

He's wearing a large raincoat and a large hat.

She's wearing a pair of baggy casual trousers and a small hat.

He's wearing small pajamas.

⭐ 1. 看完班哲文和潘朵拉的時裝表演後，你最喜歡哪件衣服？從班哲文和潘朵拉的時裝表演裏選一件，先看着圖畫說出該衣服的英文名稱；然後把圖畫蓋住，自己再說一遍。

⭐ 2. 裙子的英文名稱是什麼？

! too large　太大
too small　太小

This T-shirt is too large for me.

That T-shirt is too large for him.

答案：2. skirt

19

〈到外地去公幹〉

柏蒂‧活力鼠正在收拾行李，她要往海豚灣去寫一篇有關當地的文章。海豚灣距離巨杉山谷不遠，那裏住着她的家人。

柏蒂：長褲、襯衣和外套……都帶齊了。

潘朵拉：柏蒂阿姨，不要忘了帶你的機票啊！

Geronimo Stilton is afraid of flying, nevertheless he has decided to go with his friend Patty Spring.

Aren't you afraid of flying, Geronimo?

Uhm... yes, I'm a little afraid...

謝利連摩最怕坐飛機，然而他卻決定和他的朋友柏蒂一起去。

菲：謝利連摩，你不是最怕坐飛機的嗎？

謝利連摩：唔⋯⋯是的，我是有點害怕⋯⋯

Tell me, Tea...what should I wear on the trip?

Let's have a look in the wardrobe...

謝利連摩：菲，告訴我，我這次去應該帶些什麼衣服呢？

菲：我們先打開衣櫃看看⋯⋯

You should wear a pair of trousers, a jacket and a tie...

菲：你應該帶一條長褲、一件外套和一條領帶⋯⋯

But you should also pack your jeans, three T-shirts and a hat.

菲：還有牛仔褲、三件T恤和一頂帽子。

這時，班哲文和賴皮來到房間。
班哲文：謝利連摩叔叔，你要去哪兒？

賴皮：你要去度假嗎？

謝利連摩：是這樣的，我要和柏蒂一起去公幹。
班哲文：真的？那是不是很刺激的？

菲：但是，你要先收拾好行李。

菲幫謝利連摩收拾好行李了。這時，謝利連摩接到一個來電。

賴皮：是不是柏蒂來接你一起去呢？
謝利連摩：嗯，她正在坐的士……來接我一起去機場。

賴皮：機場？但是你最害怕坐飛機呀！
謝利連摩：唔……我以前怕，但現在不怕了！

菲：謝利連摩，再見呀！祝你旅途愉快！
賴皮：不要忘記帶你的帽子呀！

TEST 小測驗

⭐ 1. 用英語説出下面這些衣服的名稱。

(a) 領帶	(b) 西裝	(c) 帽子	(d) 裙子	(e) 雨衣
(f) 長褲	(g) 大衣	(h) 襪子	(i) 毛衣	(j) 圍巾
(k) 襯衫	(l) 背心內衣	(m) 長袖運動衫	(n) 連衣裙	(o) 皮帶

⭐ 2. 看看下面的圖畫，這些是什麼衣服？它們是什麼顏色的呢？請用英語説出來。

(a)   (b)    (c)   (d)

a pair of yellow ...   a ... ...   a pair of .. ....   an ... ...

⭐ 3. 讀出下面的衣服名稱，它們對應的中文是什麼呢？説説看。

(a) anorak	(b) sweatshirt	(c) tracksuit
(d) shorts	(e) boots	(f) tennis shoes

⭐ 4. 看看下面的圖畫，如果圖畫旁邊的句子是對的，你就説TRUE；如果不對，你就説 FALSE。

(a)  These are dungarees.

(b)   This is a skirt.

⭐ 5. 看看潘朵拉今天穿了什麼衣服，找出適當的句子，並讀出來。

(a) Pandora is wearing a green sweatshirt and a blue skirt.

(b) Pandora is wearing a blue sweatshirt and a pair of jeans.

⭐ 6. 用英語説出下面的句子。

班哲文穿着一件大雨衣和戴着一頂大帽子。

Track 4

DICTIONARY 詞典

（英、粵、普發聲）

A

a pair of　　一對

afraid　　害怕

again　　再一次

airport　　機場

anorak　　禦寒外套

article　　文章

aunt　　阿姨

B

bag　　手袋

belt　　皮帶

bike helmet　　單車頭盔

black　　黑色

blouse　　短身上衣（女性）

blue　　藍色

boots　　靴子

brown　　棕色

C

can　　能夠

cap　　鴨舌帽

cardigan　　羊毛外衣

casual trousers　　休閒褲

clothes　　衣服

clothes-horse　　晾衣架

coat　　大衣

come　　來

congratulations　　恭喜

D

decided　　決定

dolphin　　海豚

dress　　連衣裙

dressing gown

　　晨褸（普：晨袍）

dungarees　　工人褲

25

E

exciting　　刺激

F

family　　家庭

far　　遙遠

fashion show　　時裝表演

first　　首先

fly　　飛

forget　　忘記

friend　　朋友

G

green　　綠色

grey　　灰色

H

hat　　帽子

have to　　必須

help　　幫忙

her　　她的

his　　他的

I

in the meantime　　這時

interesting　　有趣的

iron　　熨斗

ironing board　　熨衣板

J

jacket　　外套

jeans　　牛仔褲

jersey　　毛織緊身上衣

judo suit　　柔道服

K

knickers　　女性內褲

L

large　　大的

laundry basket　　洗衣籃

leave　　離開

leotard　　緊身連衣褲
　　　（跳舞或做體操時穿着）

L

live　　居住

M

miniskirt　　迷你裙

my　　我的

N

nevertheless　　然而

O

on holiday　　度假

orange　　橙色

P

pajamas　　睡衣

photos　　照片

pink　　粉紅色

play　　玩耍

purple　　紫色

R

raincoat　　雨衣

really　　真的

receives　　接到

red　　紅色

report　　報告

room　　房間

S

scarf　　圍巾

shirt　　恤衫（普：襯衫）

shoes　　鞋子

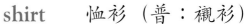

shorts　　短褲

skirt　裙子

slippers　拖鞋

small　小的

socks　襪子

sports　運動

suit　西裝

suitcase　旅行袋

sweater　毛衣

sweatshirt　長袖運動衫

T

taxi　的士

telephone call　打電話

tell　告訴

tennis shoes　網球運動鞋

ticket　機票

tie　領帶

tights　襪褲（普：褲襪）

today　今天

tracksuit　田徑服

trip　旅程

trousers　長褲

T-shirt　T恤（普：汗衫）

U

underpants　男性內褲

V

valley　山谷

vest　背心內衣

W

waistcoat　西裝背心

wardrobe　衣櫃

wash　洗

washing line　晾衣繩

washing machine　洗衣機

wear　穿

where　哪裏

white　白色

write　寫

Y

yellow　黃色

28

看在一千塊莫澤雷勒乳酪的份上，你學得開心嗎？很開心，對不對？好極了！跟你一起跳舞唱歌我也很開心！我等着你下次繼續跟班哲文和潘朵拉一起玩一起學英語呀。現在要說再見了，當然是用英語說啦！

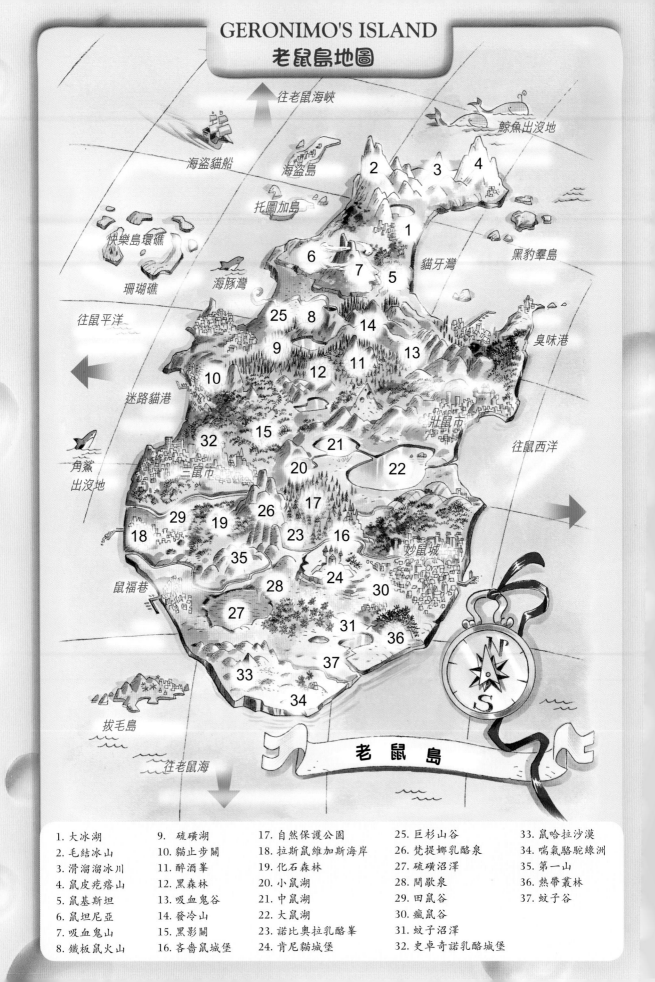

GERONIMO'S ISLAND
老鼠島地圖

往老鼠海峽

鯨魚出沒地

海盜貓船

海盜島

托圖加島

快樂島環礁

珊瑚礁　　海豚灣

貓牙灣

黑豹羣島

往鼠平洋

臭味港

壯鼠市

往鼠西洋

迷路貓港

角鯊
出沒地

三鼠市

鼠福巷

妙鼠城

老　鼠　島

拔毛島

往老鼠海

Geronimo Stilton

EXERCISE BOOK

練習冊

想知道自己對 MY CLOTHES 掌握了多少，
趕快打開後面的練習完成它吧！

ENGLISH!

5 MY CLOTHES　我的衣服

CLOTHES AND COLOURS
衣物和顏色

⭐ 根據下面每幅圖畫旁邊的文字，把各衣物填上適當的顏色。

1.

a green T-shirt

2.

a pair of red shoes

3.

a yellow hat

4.

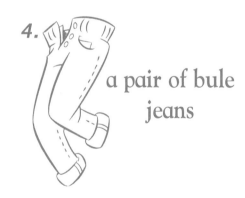

a pair of bule jeans

5.

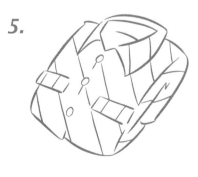

a purple shirt

6.

a pink skirt

WHAT ARE THEY WEARING?
他們穿着什麼？

⭐ 謝利連摩和他的朋友們穿着的是什麼衣物？在橫線上用英文寫出衣物的名稱。

1. _____

2. _____

3. _____

4. _____

5. _____

6. _____

7. _____

READ AND COLOUR

⭐ 讀出下面的句子，並根據句子的內容，給圖畫填上顏色。

1. He's wearing an orange shirt, a red tie and a pair of yellow trousers.

2. She's wearing a yellow jacket, a red blouse, a long blue skirt and a pair of brown shoes.

3. He's wearing a red T-shirt, a black waistcoat, a yellow coat and a pair of blue trousers.

4. She's wearing a grey dress, a red cardigan and a pair of pink shoes.

CROSSWORD PUZZLES
字母迷宮

⭐ 根據圖畫，完成下面的字母迷宮。

1.

2.

.4

3.

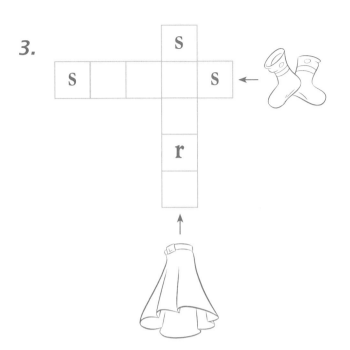

4.

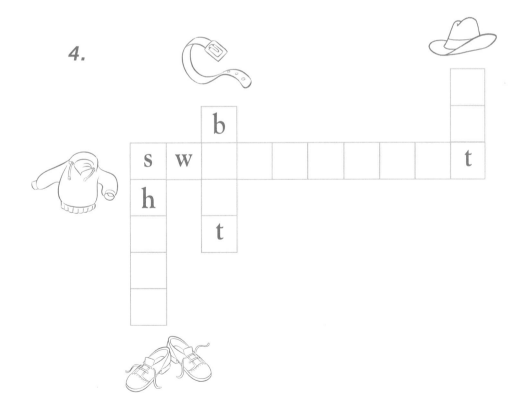

TRUE OR FALSE 分辨對與錯

⭐ 看看下面的圖畫，他們說得對嗎？如果說得對，就把TRUE的格子填上顏色；如果說得不對，就把FALSE的格子填上顏色。

1. *You are wearing a nice skirt.*
   TRUE
   FALSE

2. *You are wearing a suit.*
   TRUE
   FALSE

3. *I'm wearing my T-shirt and my jeans.*
   TRUE
   FALSE

4. *I'm wearing my tracksuit.*
   TRUE
   FALSE

5. *I'm wearing my shorts.*
   TRUE
   FALSE

6. *I'm wearing my hat.*
   TRUE
   FALSE

7.

I'm washing my shoes.
- TRUE
- FALSE

I'm washing my pajamas.
- TRUE
- FALSE

8.

This T-shirt is too large for me.
- TRUE
- FALSE

This T-shirt is too small for me.
- TRUE
- FALSE

9.

These pajamas are too large for me.
- TRUE
- FALSE

These pajamas are too small for me.
- TRUE
- FALSE

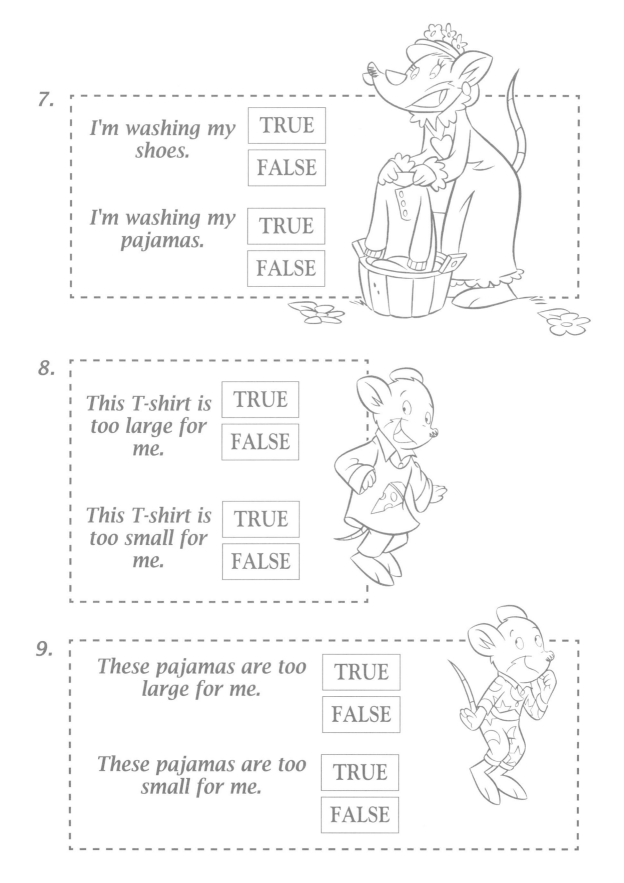

ANSWERS 答案

TEST 小測驗

1. (a)tie　(b)suit　(c)hat　(d)skirt　(e)raincoat　(f)trousers　(g)coat　(h)socks
   (i)sweater　(j)scarf　(k)shirt　(l)vest　(m)sweatshirt　(n)dress　(o) belt
2. (a) boots　(b) red anorak　(c) green trousers　(d) orange sweatshirt
3. (a) 禦寒外套　(b) 長袖運動衫　(c) 田徑服　(d) 短褲　(e) 靴子　(f) 網球運動鞋
4. (a) TRUE　(b) FALSE
5. (b) Pandora is wearing a blue sweatshirt and a pair of jeans.
6. Benjamin is wearing a big raincoat and a big hat.

EXERCISE BOOK 練習冊

P.1 略

P.2

1. jacket　　2. T-shirt　　3. shoes　　4. tie　　5. shirt　　6. trousers　　7. raincoat

P.3
略

P.4-5

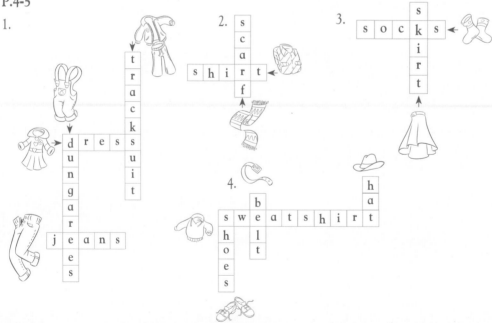

P.6-7

1. FALSE　　2. FALSE　　3. TRUE　　4. TRUE　　5. FALSE
6. FALSE　　7. FALSE, TRUE　　8. TRUE, FALSE　　9. FALSE, TRUE